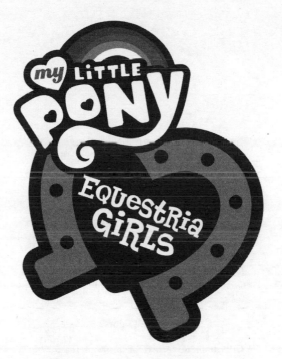

Rainbow Rocks

Written by Perdita Finn

ORCHARD

ORCHARD BOOKS
338 Euston Road, London NW1 3BH
Orchard Books Australia
Level 17/207 Kent Street, Sydney, NSW 2000

First published in 2013 in the United States
by Little, Brown and Company

This edition published by Orchard Books in 2015

HASBRO and its logo, MY LITTLE PONY, EQUESTRIA GIRLS and all
related characters are trademarks of Hasbro and are used with
permission.

A CIP catalogue record for this book is available
from the British Library.

ISBN 978 1 40833 700 4

1 3 5 7 9 10 8 6 4 2

Printed in Great Britain

MIX
Paper from
responsible sources
FSC® C104740
www.fsc.org

The paper and board used in this book are made from wood from
responsible sources.

Orchard Books is an imprint of Hachette Children's Group and
published by The Watts Publishing Group Limited, an Hachette UK
company

www.hachette.co.uk

For all the rainbow
rockers on the rise

Contents

✶ ✶ ✶

CHAPTER 1

The Ponies in the Band

Music of springtime drifted through Twilight Sparkle's open window. She could hear the bees buzzing amid the clover, the birds chirping in their new nests, and all her favourite friends whinnying and laughing as they romped together outside on the fresh green grass of Equestria.

Twilight gazed out the window. Rainbow Dash leaped into the air, showing off her newest jump in the garden. Fluttershy was quietly nibbling some daisies. Rarity was prancing so the ribbons and streamers of her hat wafted in the warm breeze, and Applejack was singing a happy springtime song.

"With my best friends, we can depend – they will always follow through. There's a guarantee of fun when I spend time with you!"

Twilight Sparkle smiled. It was good to be home after all her adventures in the human world of Canterlot High. She touched the tiara on her head with its Element of Harmony. It was nice to have her magic crown back, too. Still, she couldn't help but miss those teen girls, so similar to the ponies she knew and loved, but each special in her own human way. Twilight Sparkle wondered what those girls were doing right then. She knew that

Canterlot High always held a springtime carnival. Maybe her friends were there. Maybe handsome Flash Sentry was playing his guitar on the stage. Maybe those girls there were singing, too, just like her friends here.

There would be a Ferris wheel, a mini roller coaster, and a carousel with painted ponies set up on the school grounds. There would be silly photo booths, tons of games, and all kinds of delicious things to eat. Rarity would steer her cute convertible into a parking space. Fluttershy would be squealing with delight when she saw the rides, and Twilight Sparkle would be sitting right beside her, ready to join in all the festive fun.

Twilight Sparkle could imagine it so perfectly that her daydream almost felt real...

Rarity glanced in the rearview mirror and smoothed one of her lush, dark locks into place. She wanted to look fabulous for Canterlot High's Spring Carnival! She was wearing her favourite outfit – diamonds sparkled on her pretty skirt, her trendy boots, and even in her wavy hair. Out the rearview mirror, she caught a glance of more of her favourite friends arriving.

Applejack and Rainbow Dash were racing each other on their scooters along the pavement. When Applejack saw Rarity and Fluttershy, she took off her cowboy hat and waved it at them. "Howdy, gals!"

With a quick twist of the handlebars, Canterlot High's all-star athlete, Rainbow Dash, brought her scooter to an expert stop on the grass. *"Hanging with my friends!"* she said. She pulled her phone out of her pocket and took a photo of her friends in the convertible.

"Setting all the trends!" answered Rarity, turning it into a song.

"Check this sweet emoticon," harmonised Rainbow Dash, pushing a button to send all the girls a copy of the photo.

"Hi, everyone! Aren't the Carnival decorations the best ever? I helped make the streamers extra sparkly!" Pinkie Pie pedalled over on her glittery bike, enthusiastically honking her horn.

The girls hopped out of the car, and Rarity continued singing, *"With my best friends, though we're different, we feel like we still belong, and every day it makes our friendship..."*

"Strong!" they sang together.

They linked arms and continued singing together as they pranced towards the Carnival.

"Running round all through the day, singing music that we play. There is never time for rest, because my friends are the best!"

DJ Pon-3 was passing by on her way to spin some discs for the festivities when Rainbow Dash got a text. "'You girls sound pretty good. Ever think of making a band?'" Rainbow read aloud. DJ Pon-3 pulled down her high-fashion shades and winked at them.

Fluttershy giggled, embarrassed. Rarity looked surprised. Pinkie Pie squealed with delight. Applejack nodded her head, seriously considering the suggestion, and Rainbow Dash beamed the happiest smile of all. "That's a great idea!"

"A band? Did someone mention a

band? I'm going to start a band and I'm going to be the star because the Great and Powerful Trixie is the most fantastic singer of all!" Trixie flounced past the girls, her nose in the air, without even stopping to say hello.

"It takes a special kind of magic to make a band come together," said Applejack.

"What kind of magic is that?" asked Fluttershy.

"The kind we have!" said Applejack. "The Magic of Friendship!"

"The important thing is to sing and have fun!" said Pinkie Pie. And that's what she did as the other girls joined in.

"Running round all through the day, singing music that we play. There is never time for rest, because my friends are the best!"

Their first stop was the carousel. Each

girl hopped on a horse just as the music began. Up and down, up and down, and round and round they rode!

"Giddyup!" said Rarity.

"Yeehaw!" exclaimed Applejack.

Fluttershy stroked the mane of her carousel pony. She loved every kind of animal. Pinkie Pie was surprised to find that her pink pony looked just like her! Rarity took out her phone and started making a video of her friends.

The girls were having such a good time!

"Posting videos online of us goofing all the time. Friends like these are super cool, 'cause my friends they really RULE!" they sang.

Then they took a ride on the roller coaster, and the girls screamed as it whipped around turns and plunged down hills. Still breathless after they got off, they ran over to get some candyfloss. Pinkie Pie posed for a photo with hers. It looked just like her hair! Pinkie Pie couldn't resist a decorating moment. She grabbed a handful of sweets, sticking jelly beans onto her funnel of candyfloss so they looked like eyes and using a string of liquorice to look like a mouth.

Rainbow Dash took a photo of Pinkie Pie with her candyfloss creation!

From a booth decorated with streamers, DJ Pon-3 was playing music for the Carnival. There was music everywhere, and the girls couldn't stop singing. There was just so much to do.

Applejack and Rainbow Dash couldn't resist the dunk tank, but they were both so good at pitching that every ball they threw hit the mark – and splashed a person into the water. Next they raced over to a ring toss game and won an adorable stuffed bunny. They gave it to Fluttershy as a gift, and she loved it.

Fluttershy and Pinkie Pie were having a blast at the photo centre. Fluttershy stuck her head through a hole in a piece of plywood, and from the other side it looked like she was now a lovable bear. Pinkie Pie stuck her head through a different hole, and she was transformed into a clown. Rarity instantly texted the photos to Applejack and Rainbow Dash.

Rarity was examining herself in the fun-house mirror. She looked so weird – and that's exactly when Rainbow Dash snapped a photo of her. Rarity chased after her, screaming and laughing!

"Texting kinda gets confused," Rarity began singing when she grabbed Rainbow Dash's phone.

"*But we always are amused,*" sang Rainbow Dash.

"*My friends stand out in a crowd, having fun and laughing loud,*" crooned the other girls, coming close and trying to get a peek at the funny photo of Rarity.

Trixie walked by with an ice-cream cone and glanced at the girls. "I wouldn't let my friends take ugly pictures of me," she said.

"Oh, Trixie," said Pinkie Pie. "It's all silliness. Come take photos with us in the photo booth." But Trixie didn't want to.

The day was a flurry of activity. Applejack and Rainbow Dash both fished for prizes and won a stuffed cat for Rarity. Then at the high striker they were both so good at hitting the bell with the hammer that they won prizes for all their friends! They took tons of funny photos of one another, and through it all, they never stopped singing.

"With my best friends, we can depend – they will always follow through. There's a guarantee of fun when I spend time with you!"

DJ Pon-3 had been watching – and listening to – the girls all day from her booth. They really had something special. She texted Rainbow Dash.

"Remember what I said about a band?"

"We sure do!" said Rainbow Dash as she typed out her response. "I've decided we're going to make it happen!"

"Do you think you could get one together in time for the Spring Fling?" DJ Pon-3 wrote back.

"The Spring Fling?" said Rainbow Dash. "That's a magical night."

"What would we have to do?" asked Fluttershy.

"Practise hard," said Rainbow Dash, thinking about what she always did to prepare for her sporting events.

"Write some songs," said Applejack.

"Get instruments," said Pinkie Pie.

"And learn how to play them," said Fluttershy, worried.

"And create fantabulous outfits for us to wear!" exclaimed Rarity. "Let's do it, girls!"

"Spring Fling, here we come!" said Rainbow Dash.

"Is it going to be a Battle of the Bands?" said Trixie, suddenly appearing beside them. "Because if it is, I'm going to win."

"You can be in our band, if you want," said Rarity.

"Your band? Your band doesn't have room for me. The Great and Powerful Trixie is going to be her own one-gal band, and she's going to be the star! Just you wait and see."

"Do we have to be stars?" said Fluttershy nervously.

"Not at all," said Applejack. "We just have to have fun."

"And practise," Rainbow Dash reminded her.

"And practise," agreed all the girls.

"Let's do one more photo, girls. For the band!" gushed Pinkie Pie.

All the girls crammed into the photo booth. What a picture! Shining eyes, smiling mouths, and so many colours of hair!

Twilight Sparkle wondered if she'd ever get a chance to return to Canterlot High.

Now that the magic mirror was gone, she probably wouldn't. But she hoped that her human friends were happy and that they'd always remember her, just like she remembered them.

She sang a special Carnival Day song for them, wherever they were and whatever they were doing.

"With my best friends,
Though we're different,
We feel like we still belong,
And every day it makes our friendship,
STRONG!

"With my best friends,
We can depend,
They will always follow through.
There's a guarantee of fun,
When I spend time with YOU!"

There was a knock on the door, and Flash Sentry poked his head into the room.

"Excuse me, Princess," he said. "I couldn't help but notice your singing. You're good enough to have your own band!"

Twilight Sparkle blushed right down to her unicorn horn. "Maybe someday…"

What Twilight Sparkle didn't know was just how real her daydream was. Back at Canterlot High, her friends really were starting a band – and one day she might even be in it!

Chapter 2

Guitar Centred

Rainbow Dash woke up on a beautiful spring morning. She'd had a dream of all the girls singing together onstage. Rainbow Dash knew that they were supposed to start making music together. But first she needed to get herself a new guitar! That's why she was dragging everyone to the Music Centre after school.

"I simply don't understand why you can't just play the guitar you have," sighed

Rarity, looking at the guitar case Rainbow Dash was carrying.

Rainbow Dash shook her head, put the guitar case on the floor, and opened it. Inside was an old, beat-up guitar. It wasn't just dusty and well worn; it was broken. One of the tuners was missing, and a mess of snapped strings curled around the guitar's neck like cobwebs.

"Ew!" exclaimed Rarity. "Now I understand."

"I guess it's been a while since you took that guitar out for a ride," said Applejack.

"I used to practise a lot," said Rainbow Dash. "But then I got so busy with soccer and basketball and swimming and..."

DJ Pon-3 looked up from the cashier's desk and sent a text: "You girls are starting a band, I see."

"We are," said Rarity. "We really want

to perform at the Spring Fling. But now we've got to figure out what everyone's going to play."

Pinkie Pie was bouncing around the store checking out all the different kinds of instruments. There were mandolins and violins, giant cellos and upright basses, banjos and ukuleles. But most of all there were guitars: acoustic guitars made of soft, polished wood and dazzling electric guitars in every shape and colour. There were square guitars, triangular guitars, and even guitars shaped like stars.

"How 'bout this one? How 'bout this one?" said Pinkie Pie enthusiastically, plinking the string of a black electric guitar decorated with orange and red flames. "Or this?" She picked up a sparkling blue guitar and began dancing around with it like she was a rock-and-roll star. Almost immediately, though, she dropped it when she caught sight of a tiny little guitar for a child. "Ooooh! Lookie here! Lookie here!"

"No, Pinkie!" Rainbow Dash laughed as her friend zoomed around the store.

Now Pinkie had found an Indian sitar, which had a round head and a long, long neck. "Check this out!" she called to Rainbow. "You like?"

"No, Pinkie."

"How about this? This is super groovy!" She picked up a blue-and-purple electric guitar shaped like a butterfly.

Rainbow shook her head. She was carefully studying a whole wall of guitars.

"Well, whatcha lookin' for, Rainbow?" asked Applejack.

"That's the problem. I need to find something that *looks* as awesome as I'm gonna make it sound."

Rarity had wandered over to the keyboard section of the store and was trying out one of the pianos.

"You play beautifully," said Fluttershy softly. "I wish I knew how to play an instrument."

"You don't have to play an instrument," said Rarity reassuringly. "You can sing. I've heard you. We're going to need lots of singing in our band!"

"Okay," said Fluttershy. But still she looked worried. It was fun to think about being in a band, but it was scary, too. Every time she thought about performing onstage, she felt really nervous.

"What about this one?!" shouted Pinkie Pie.

"That's a bass guitar," said Applejack, taking a look at it. "A nice one, too. But I already got one at home for me to play."

Rainbow Dash sighed. She liked to have good equipment when she played – whether it was the perfect pair of shorts, a brand-new ball, or a guitar that would let her fingers create just the right music for their band.

She studied each guitar on the wall one more time. She looked at the guitars hanging from the ceiling. She looked at pink guitars, blue guitars, old guitars and new guitars. And then she saw it. On a stand. In the corner. It was the most perfect guitar she had ever seen. It had flair, it had style, but best of all, it was decorated with tiny, shiny rainbows.

Rainbow Dash's jaw dropped; her eyes lit up. Of course! This was what she had been looking for. She ran over to it. She couldn't wait to play it! It was calling to her! Already, she could feel music pouring through her. She reached out to take it in her hands, and just as she did, another hand grabbed hold of it.

It was Trixie!

"Hands off my guitar, Trixie!" shouted Rainbow Dash. She pulled the guitar towards her.

"I touched it first, Rainbow Dash!" screamed Trixie, yanking the guitar back in her direction.

The girls were just about to begin a full-out tug-of-war when Applejack ran over. "Simmer down there, ladies," she ordered.

But neither girl took her hand off the rainbow guitar.

"There's no need to become ruffians," said Rarity, "when a simple inquiry could solve the problem."

She trotted over to the cashier's desk to talk to DJ Pon-3. "Excuse me, but do you happen to have this same exact guitar in the back, and if so, could I trouble you to get it for me, please?"

DJ Pon-3's eyes narrowed as she looked at the guitar the two girls were fighting over. The girls looked back at her, hopeful. All the friends crowded around. Other customers in the store stopped what they were doing to listen to the answer.

DJ Pon-3 shook her head.

"Oh," said Rarity, disappointed.

Rainbow's hand reached up higher on the neck of the guitar to grab hold of it tighter. Trixie's hand tightened its grasp, too.

"Now what?" said Rainbow Dash. There was no way she was letting go. This was her guitar. Couldn't Trixie see that?

Applejack took off her cowboy hat and scratched her head, thinking out loud. "Well, there's one guitar and two gals who want it."

Everyone was looking at her expectantly.

"Sounds to me," said Applejack, rubbing her hands together in anticipation, "like this has the makin's for a nice, friendly competition."

Rainbow's eyes lit up! She loved a tournament. "Yeah!" she shouted. "Whatcha wanna play, Trixie? Baseball, basketball, soccer?"

Rainbow winked at Fluttershy. "I'll totally crush her, and this guitar will be mine!"

"That doesn't sound nice or friendly," said Fluttershy.

Trixie looked irritated. "Seriously,

Rainbow? You are the best athlete at Canterlot High. We can compete, but it has to be something that the Great and Powerful Trixie is good at, too."

All the girls rolled their eyes. Trixie was so full of herself sometimes!

But Rainbow Dash was smiling. "Well, Great and Powerful Trixie, seein' as we both want this guitar…let's see who plays the best!"

"A shred-off?" said Trixie, looking concerned for the first time.

Rainbow smiled confidently. "Shred ON!"

CHAPTER 3

Duelling Guitars

DJ Pon-3 came out from behind the counter and took the prized rainbow guitar, holding it above Rainbow Dash and Trixie. She had let them know they could pick any guitar in the store for the shred-off, but this was the prize for the winner.

Rainbow Dash selected a simple electric guitar from a nearby stand and plugged it into an amp. She put the strap around her neck and began warming up her fingers with a few quick scales and chords.

Trixie chose the guitar that looked like a butterfly and almost instantly her fingers were flying across the strings, creating an irresistible rift.

"I sure hope our Rainbow is up to speed," whispered Applejack to Rarity.

"Shh!" said Fluttershy. "She's going to do great. We just have to believe in her."

Trixie dazzled the crowd with electrifying playing. She had style and energy. She was awesome. Kids in the crowd had started clapping along while she played.

But Rainbow was determined, and she was sliding and bending notes to create all kinds of wild effects. The girls' licks grew more and more complex and powerful, astounding the audience with their righteous riffs and mind-boggling power chords.

Trixie dropped to one knee and let loose with out of this world strumming. Her dark hair was flying, she had her eyes shut, and every cell in her body seemed to be focused on her playing.

Cries of "Whoa! Yeah! Go, Trixie!" rose up from the crowd. She was mighty! Everyone was hollering and applauding.

For a moment, Rainbow Dash glanced up from her playing. Was she going to lose? Did she have it in her to wow the crowd? She looked around the store and saw her friends. They were counting on her. She had to do it for the Equestria Girls. She had to.

A determined expression came over her face as she totally went for it with a dazzling run of notes. Her fingers were racing, the strings were dancing, music was pouring out of the guitar. She made it sound like a waterfall, a thunderstorm, and then the sun bursting through the clouds after the rain. The music was irresistible. Her friends started singing along as she played.

"Hey, hey, everybody,
We're here to shout,
That the Magic of Friendship,
Is what it's all about!"

Rainbow Dash was strutting across the floor of the Music Centre, jamming her guitar. She shook her head, and her colourful mane of hair danced as she played. She lifted up her knees, dancing and prancing. And that's when the magic happened! She had pony ears and a pony tail! She was going to pony up!

"Heavens!" exclaimed Rarity.

"Good gravy!" said Applejack.

"Oh my!" Fluttershy was stunned.

"Whoa! Check me out!" shouted Rainbow Dash over the music. She wasn't just a rock and roller, she was a full-fledged pony player!

Trixie stopped playing. She couldn't believe it. How could she even compete with that?

Rainbow Dash leaped into the air, gave one last triumphant strum to her guitar, and landed, breathless, transformed back into herself, in the middle of the Music Centre.

The crowd went wild, screaming, cheering, and applauding. "Rainbow Dash! Rainbow Dash!" They shouted her name over and over again. There was no question about it. Trixie was an amazing player, but Rainbow Dash was the winner.

DJ Pon-3 pushed through the crowd, the prized guitar in her hands, and handed it to Rainbow Dash. Trixie was furious. She threw down the guitar she'd been playing and stomped her feet. "No, no, no, no, no!!!!" she screamed, throwing a temper tantrum. Her hands were balled up into fists, and her face was bright red. "The Great and Powerful Trixie does not accept this! You shall all rue the day!" She looked like she was about to explode.

Rainbow Dash studied the guitar DJ Pon-3 had just given her. It was certainly stylish, but that wasn't what made a guitar sound great. And it was the sound that mattered when you came right down to it.

"Eh." Rainbow Dash shrugged. "You

can have it." She handed Trixie the guitar.

Trixie clutched the guitar close to her chest as if Rainbow Dash might instantly change her mind.

But Rainbow Dash was looking at the simple blue guitar she'd just played. *You should never choose your friends by how they look*, she thought to herself. What mattered was that you could make music together. This guitar might not look like anything special, but it was magic. "Turns out this is the one that speaks to me," she said, smiling.

DJ Pon-3 gave her a thumbs-up and went over to the cash register to ring it up. Rainbow Dash took out her purse and handed over a small wad of bills.

"It's your loss," said Trixie.

"I doubt it," said Rainbow Dash.

With the guitar paid for, Rainbow Dash

slung it over her shoulder. Now it was time to get some real practice in before the Spring Fling. There was no telling what kind of music she could make once all the girls started playing together.

As the girls headed out of the store, they overheard Trixie talking to DJ Pon-3. "Twelve hundred dollars?! What do you mean twelve hundred dollars?! For a guitar! You'll pay for this, Rainbow Dash!" she shouted.

Pinkie Pie giggled. "No, silly. If you want it, *you'll* have to pay for it!"

CHAPTER 4

Springtime's Soundtrack

DJ Pon-3 couldn't get Rainbow Dash's guitar playing out of her head. On the way to school the next day, every noise she heard was like an accompaniment to her friend's amazing music.

As she stood at the street corner waiting for the light to change, every sound seemed to be harmonising with the tune in her head. Speeding cars whizzed past at regular intervals like the thump of a bass;

the footsteps of people hurrying on their way to work became a steady rhythm section; a bus's sudden honking was a trumpet; some children's laughter, the tinkling disks of a tambourine.

She could just imagine the band the Equestria Girls could create. With their singing and Rainbow Dash's playing, they could really make something special happen. But did they have it in them to put a whole band together? Could they find a bass player good enough to play with Rainbow Dash? A keyboardist? A rhythm section? A drummer? It was impossible to find drummers for a band. Everyone knew that. And what's a band without a drummer?

Just then the light at the crosswalk changed. The little red stick figure on the sign that had been holding up his hand to say "stop" changed into a little green stick figure. DJ Pon-3 heard Rainbow Dash's playing again in her head and imagined that little green guy dancing up a storm to the imaginary music. Everyone would be bouncing up and down to that beat!

Music like that would get the whole world dancing. As she walked across the street, she imagined a heavy bass kicking in and everyone and everything around her grooving to the music. The old lady walking her dog would start rocking. The dogs in their jumpers would start prancing. Baby birds up in the trees would be boppin' their heads and singing along. Stray cats hissing at one another in the alley would stop yowling and start purring! The policemen would blow their whistles in time to the beat. Even the cars would start dancing to the music Rainbow

Dash had played.

Kids who had never danced would dance together if the Equestria Girls had a band. The Spring Fling would be a success! That was the magic secret of really good music – it brought people together.

DJ Pon-3 reached the other side of the street determined to help the girls in any way she could to make their band happen. She didn't see it, but just behind her, the little green stick figure on the crosswalk sign waved his arms and did a moonwalk in celebration. Music really was magic!

CHAPTER 5

The Case of the Missing Bass

After watching Rainbow Dash's amazing performance, Applejack was eager to get her old bass guitar out of her grandmother's cupboard so she could start jamming with her friends. The bass is a little longer and bigger than a regular guitar, and it gives a band its rhythm. That's the way Applejack thought of herself, honestly, not as the star but the girl who helped everyone keep their rhythm.

But Applejack was not feeling very happy when she and the rest of the ponies got to Granny Smith's house. Her bass wasn't in the cupboard where she'd left it. She searched the whole house, but she couldn't find it anywhere. Where was it? That's when Granny told her that she had thought it was junk and got rid of it just the other day at her car boot sale! Now what was Applejack going to do? They couldn't have a band without a bass player. She had to find a way to get her bass back. There was no way she could afford another one. They were expensive.

But surely if she explained all this to the person who had bought it at Granny Smith's car boot sale, they would understand and give it back to her? It was the only thing she could do. There was only one problem. Could Granny Smith remember who had bought it?

"OK, Granny, one more time, when you accidentally sold my bass, who did you sell it to?" Applejack was upset, but she was trying not to lose her temper with her grandmother.

Granny Smith's brow wrinkled. She shut her eyes. She opened them. She shook her head. She just couldn't remember.

"Was it a man or a woman?" asked Applejack.

"It was definitely a woman," said Granny, smiling.

Applejack nodded. "OK, that's a start."

Granny Smith twisted her apron between her hands. Her brow was furrowed again. "Did I say woman? I meant man."

Applejack gave an exasperated whinny

and looked like she was about to scream. Quickly, Rainbow Dash jumped in. It looked like the girls were going to have to do some supersleuthing before they could even begin to practise as a band.

"Granny," she asked, "did the man who took the bass say *why* he wanted it? Was he a musician?"

Granny Smith looked surprised. "A magician? What would a magician want with your old boots?"

Applejack exploded with frustration. "Not my boots. My BASS!" she shouted.

"Now there's no need to shout," said Granny Smith. "I remember exactly who I sold your bass to. I thought we were talking about your boots. I sold your bass to a couple of brothers."

The girls all looked relieved at Granny's confidence.

"Slim and Slam. Those were their names," said Granny.

Fluttershy took out a notebook and wrote down the names of the brothers, but almost instantaneously she had to cross them out.

"Or was it Trim and Tram?" said Granny. "Nope. That's not it. Skim and Skam?"

All the girls were leaning in and listening, hopeful.

"Granny, please try to remember," begged Applejack. "We're going to perform at the Spring Fling, but only if I can find my bass. Are you sure it was Skim and Skam?"

Granny shook her head, and all the girls sighed like deflated balloons. "Hold on!" said Granny. "It's coming to me. I think I've got it. It was Flim and Flam."

Rarity pulled out her phone and did a search on Flim and Flam. "That's it!" she said. "They own a thrift shop right near Canterlot High!"

"Now we just have to hope no one's already bought it!" said Rainbow Dash.

"Quick, gals," said Applejack. "There's no time to lose!"

CHAPTER 6

Rock-and-Roll Hall of Shame!

The Flim Flam brothers were dressed in matching suits with blue-and-white-striped shirts and matching grey bow ties. They each wore a straw boater, askew on the top of their slicked-down hair. When the girls rushed breathlessly into their shop, they were just putting Applejack's bass in the display case in the front window.

"Welcome to the grand opening of the

Flim Flam Brothers' Everything under the Sun Emporium," they said together, doffing their hats with a flourish and bowing slightly to the girls.

"You want it, we got it," said Flam.

"Need a pogo stick?" offered Flim. Immediately he produced one, hopped onto it, and began jumping around the store.

The girls, a little overwhelmed, didn't know what to say.

"How about a bowling ball?" asked Flam. He took one from a shelf and sent it rolling across the floor, where it hit a stack of bowling pins and knocked them over.

"Want a stuffed clown?" Flim's arm was around a giant stuffed clown with a red nose and curly hair.

"Want...whatever this is?" Flam couldn't figure out what he was holding, and neither could the girls.

Applejack stepped forward. "I'll take that bass."

The girls all looked relieved as Flam took the bass out of the window and showed it to Applejack. It was a sleek, red, well-used bass. Applejack had been playing it for a long time.

"Excellent taste, young lady!" said Flim with a slimy smile. "We can give you this bass for a nonnegotiable price of one thousand dollars."

The girls gasped. "One thousand dollars!" exclaimed Rainbow Dash. "You only paid Granny Smith two dollars for it."

The girls nodded in agreement. "That's right, two dollars."

Flim and Flam exchanged glances.

Flim coughed. "Yes…well…"

"We have to cover our overheads!" said

Flam with a shrug.

"And transportation," added Flim, recovering his composure. "And of course, there's our stocking fee."

Applejack stuck her thumbs in her denim shirt and prepared for business. "Listen," she said. "This all boils down to a simple misunderstandin'. You bought that bass from my granny, but it wasn't hers to sell and I simply cannot let ya keep it." She nodded, satisfied that now everything was clear. But Applejack had a good heart, and she didn't like to be unfair to anyone. "I'll tell you what. I'll give you the two dollars back, and we'll call it even Stephen."

Applejack reached into her pocket and pulled out a couple of carefully folded bills. She held them out with one hand and with the other reached for her bass.

But Flam quickly stepped away from her. "Your bass?" he questioned her.

"Not your granny's?" said Flim.

Flim and Flam winked at each other and laughed. "A likely story!" they said together.

Flam put the bass behind him, and the two brothers stood in front of it like a wall.

Applejack was dumbfounded. She was so honest, she was always flabbergasted when other people weren't. "It *is* a likely story," she tried to explain. "Because I'm tellin' the truth. That's my bass."

The other girls nodded their heads in agreement.

"Is that so?" said Flim. "And can you prove that this is in fact your bass?"

Applejack smiled. "Yep. For one thing, my name's Applejack, and my initials are written on the strap."

For a moment, Flim and Flam looked

concerned. They studied the bass and examined the strap. Just like Applejack had said, her initials were right there in bold lettering.

"See! See!" said the girls excitedly. Now maybe at last they could get started on practising for their band.

But Flim and Flam weren't going to give up that easily. "Come now," said Flam, "that AJ could stand for anything...Art Jerks."

"Alien Jones," said Flim.

"Anvil Jokers," suggested Flam.

"Why, I'll bet you don't even play the bass...Applejack...if that's your real name."

Applejack was madder than a bull at a rodeo at this point. "Applejack is my real name. And I do play the bass. That one." What else could she say to convince them?

And what would she do if she couldn't get her bass back? There was no way she could afford another one. What was she going to do now? She couldn't think of any other way to convince them to give it to her.

But that's what friends are for!

Rainbow Dash knew exactly the move that would solve this problem. "Go on, Applejack. Show 'em what you've got."

"Yes," said Rarity to Flim and Flam. "Give her the respect she deserves, and let her display her talents."

Rainbow Dash's eyes twinkled. "Seems like we've found the solution."

"Yes! Yes! Yes!" agreed Pinkie Pie. "You'll see how amazing and awesome and fantabulous she is! Let her play."

"I think you have to," said Fluttershy quietly. "It's only fair."

Flim and Flam looked from one girl to

another. There was no way they could say no to so many potential customers. Reluctantly, they held out the bass to Applejack. Flim coughed nervously. Flam bit his lip.

Applejack strung the guitar strap over her shoulder. "You have an amp?" she asked. When Flim and Flam produced one, she plugged in her bass. "Hold on to your ears, boys. I'm going to let it rip!"

And she did. Applejack could play! Her fingers were flying, and Flim and Flam's Emporium was rockin'! People passing by on the street stopped to peer in. This was great! What a solo! What a performance! Her rhythms were complex, precise...infectious! Everyone was tapping their feet and swaying to the music. Best of all, the Equestria Girls were singing along.

"Shake your tail 'cause we're here to have a party tonight!
Shake your tail! Shake your tail!"

And that's when the magic happened!

First the ears appeared, and then her hair began to look like a horse's mane, and then her tail was swinging and dancing while she played! She was playing pony style!

All the girls in the store started to do the Pony Stomp! They lifted their knees and pranced. They crossed their arms and leaned from side to side. They jumped out and did the Canterlot Clap! They stomped their feet and punched the air in celebration with their hands. These girls could really dance when the music was right.

Even Flim and Flam were tapping

their feet. What a beat!

As Applejack shredded one last triumphant riff, the girls all started jumping up and down. "See? See?" they said. "It is her bass!"

Applejack carefully removed her bass. She was a normal girl again.

All the girls were looking at Flim and Flam, who were still swaying to the music. Fluttershy cleared her throat.

"Oh yes, oh yes," admitted Flim. "Well, well, well. Perhaps this is her bass."

Relieved, Applejack reached back into her pocket and took out the two dollars again.

"But there are still the transportation costs," said Flim quickly.

"Don't forget the stocking fees!" added Flam.

"Wouldn't dream of it," agreed Flim.

Applejack stomped her foot in frustration. Now she wanted to play her bass with her friends more than ever. "Just tell me how much you want for it already!"

Rainbow Dash stepped forward. "And don't even think about saying a thousand dollars."

Flim pulled Flam aside for a moment, and the two brothers whispered together conspiratorially. Finally, Flam turned to Applejack, an oily smile on his lips. "I suppose," he said slowly, "we could make some kind of ... trade?"

Applejack looked at him questioningly. What did she possibly have to trade?

That was how Applejack found herself in front of the store an hour later, jamming on her bass, in a banana costume. A huge flashing neon arrow behind her pointed to the store's entrance. Well, she was certainly drawing a crowd – and she'd have her bass back at the end of the day.

"Are those the costumes for your band?" snickered Trixie when she walked by.

"Just for practisin'," said Applejack good-naturedly. After all, practice was practice, even if you did have to wear a banana suit!

CHAPTER 7

Jam Session

DJ Pon-3 was headed to the Sweet Shoppe for an afternoon treat along with some of the kids from Canterlot High. She had in her earphones and was listening to music, but she kept hearing a more insistent tune out on the street. And that's when she saw the giant performing banana!

That fruit can rock, she thought to herself. Then she realised that hidden inside the yellow costume was Applejack.

She pulled out her earphones so she could really listen.

Wow! She could imagine Applejack and Rainbow Dash strutting across the stage. It looked like the girls might be able to get this band together after all.

"Doesn't she look ridiculous?" said Trixie, coming up beside her. "I think it would ruin the Spring Fling to let anyone that silly-looking perform."

"You don't *look* at music," a text response from DJ Pon-3 said, "you listen to it! And you can't stop listening to Applejack."

"Hmmph! I can!" said Trixie. She stomped off down the street.

But as Trixie disappeared around the corner, DJ Pon-3 noticed that she was walking in time to the rhythm of the bass.

Kids were going in and out of the Sweet

Shoppe, and every one of them was moving to the music. Even the coffee glugging out of the espresso machines seemed to be harmonising with it! Kids were munching their muffins to the beat. A baby was slurping his milk bottle in rhythm. A tiny dog poking out of a lady's fancy handbag was blinking his little black eyes to it.

Standing in line, DJ Pon-3 was snapping her fingers as Applejack's awesome music pulsed through the shop. Just add a drum set, a keyboard and some vocals, and the Spring Fling was going to be unforgettable!

"Good afternoon!" said Mrs Cake from behind the counter. "What can I get for you?"

DJ Pon-3 smiled and pointed to an enormous blueberry muffin with crumble topping in the glass case. Mrs Cake leaned into the case, grabbed the muffin, and dropped it into a white paper bag, humming as she did so.

"It's a wonderful day, isn't it?" she said to DJ Pon-3.

She smiled as she handed Mrs Cake a dollar bill.

The music was reaching a crescendo, and everyone in the Sweet Shoppe was bouncing to the beat. It was like a flash mob, only it was completely unplanned. Customers found themselves doing the Pony Stomp, lifting their knees and prancing, clapping their hands, and waving their arms from side to side. They couldn't help it! The music was just too magical.

With a final riff of notes, the music came to a climactic finish. One customer who'd been waving his hands over his head lost his balance and staggered, and his smoothie tipped and spilled. But it didn't matter. Not one bit. Nothing mattered when you were dancing!

CHAPTER 8

A Walk on the Wild Side

During school the next day, Rarity noticed that Fluttershy was even quieter than usual. Whenever the girls talked about getting the band together, she seemed to disappear, playing with a lock of her pink hair or whispering something to one of the beloved pets she always carried in her pocket. Rarity decided that maybe if she spent the afternoon with her friend, she could figure out what was the matter.

Besides, it would mean that she'd get to cuddle all kinds of cute furry friends at the Animal Rescue Centre, where Fluttershy worked.

"Thanks for coming, Rarity," said Fluttershy when her friend showed up at the Centre. "We need all the help we can get."

"But of course, darling," gushed Rarity. "Helping cute little puppies and kittens will never go out of style. And if there's anything you need to talk about, you just let me know, okay?"

Fluttershy nodded, almost said something, and then changed her mind. She had so many animals to pet and greet. This wasn't a good time to tell Rarity what was bothering her. Besides, everyone else was having so much fun getting the band together. She didn't want to disappoint her friends. How could she sing onstage while Rainbow Dash and Applejack jammed on their guitars, Rarity tickled the ivories of her keyboard, and Pinkie Pie sang? How was she going to tell all her friends she just couldn't do it?

Rarity knelt down on the floor to cuddle a particularly adorable floppy-eared puppy. How hard was this for a job? Maybe she should start coming here with Fluttershy more often.

"Today we have a really special assignment," said Fluttershy eagerly.

"Do we?" said Rarity. A little kitten nuzzled its head against her arm, and she petted it.

Fluttershy adjusted the butterfly barrette in her hair. "What we're going to do today is even more special than working with the kittens. Once a year, a lucky volunteer gets to clean the Hamster Habitat."

She pointed across the room to the most enormous hamster cage Rarity had ever seen. It took up the entire length of the wall from floor to ceiling. Colourful plastic tubes crisscrossed one another in an elaborate maze. There were ladders and burrows and wheels. There were tunnels and caves and houses. And there were hamsters. Lots and lots of hamsters.

Rarity tried to hide her lack of enthusiasm. "We have to clean... *that*?"

"It's quite an honour," explained Fluttershy. "I signed up months ago to be sure I'd get it." With that, she skipped over to the Habitat. Carefully, she opened the cage door and lifted the edge of one of the plastic tubes. "Housekeeping!" she sang out happily.

A fat little brown-and-white hamster stuck his nose out of the tube. More and more little hamsters were scurrying toward Fluttershy.

Rarity shuddered and took a step away from the Habitat. "Fluttershy, darling, aren't hamsters, um, you know, um...rodents?"

"They sure are!" gushed Fluttershy. "But they are as cute and cuddly as bunnies!"

Rarity was not sure she believed her. Hamsters were emerging from tunnels and houses and wheels. A large herd of hamsters was swarming around Fluttershy's feet, and she was happily patting their little heads, tickling their twitching whiskers, and giving them welcoming kisses.

"OK, every hamster," she cooed to

them. "Follow my friend Rarity into the next room. She'll take good care of you while I give your home a scrub."

All the hamsters stared at Rarity with beady little black eyes. Rarity gulped and tried to smile. *Well*, she thought, *at least I'm not cleaning up after them.* How hard could it be to look after a herd of hamsters, anyway?

CHAPTER 9

The Pied Piper of Hamsters

Fluttershy hoped Rarity was having a good time with the hamsters. While she scrubbed and cleaned and disinfected, she decided that she would talk to Rarity about the band. Maybe Rarity would help her explain to the other girls why she couldn't be in it. When she had finally wiped dry the last maze in the Habitat, she put her cleaning supplies away, grabbed her backpack, and opened the door to the next room to bring back the hamsters.

But she was not prepared for what she saw. Not at all! Whizzing balls of fur were shooting in all directions. It was chaos! Total chaos! In the midst of it was Rarity, her hair tousled and covered in little bits of cloth. She looked as crazed as the hamsters.

"Rarity, what happened?!" asked Fluttershy, alarmed. She quickly shut the door behind her to make sure no hamster escaped.

Rarity was completely overwhelmed. She pointed at one particularly fat little hamster who had a tattered ribbon dangling from his neck. "Well, Carl Pettington's coat just begged to be accessorised, but Emilia Furhart refused to be left out." She pointed at still another hamster with a circle of cloth stuck to the top of her head. "And she got Curtis Pawpower and Mayfield Bumblepuss to chew right through Carl's little scarf, and before I knew it, I had a Habitat-wide feud on my hands." With an exhausted exhale, she collapsed on the floor, and hamsters crowded onto her lap.

Fluttershy was confused. Carl Pettington? Curtis Pawpower?

"Also, I named them," said Rarity, trying to smile.

Fluttershy clapped her hands authoritatively. "Ladies and gentle-hamsters, please!"

At the sound of Fluttershy's voice, all the hamsters became absolutely still and looked up at her.

"Now, I know you are all upset," she began. There was a cascade of chattering.

"Shh," soothed Fluttershy. "Why don't we head back over to the Habitat and talk it all out?"

The hamster with the torn ribbon around his neck staggered over to Rarity, and she instantly picked him up, cradling him in her hands. She slicked back the fur on the top of his head. "I mean, honestly," she cooed at him. "Not every hamster can expect to look as smart in a scarf as Carl here."

Carl Pettington's furry white chest puffed out with pride. Then he stuck out his tongue at the other hamsters. Immediately they all set to squabbling again. They chittered! They bickered! They bit!

"Stop that!" ordered Fluttershy, but they weren't listening to her anymore. She shook her head and scolded Rarity. "That wasn't exactly helpful. How are we ever going to get them back into their Habitat?"

Rarity found a tiny little hamster-sized dress she had made and held it up. A hamster lifted its head curiously. Slowly, Rarity led the hamster to the door, opened it, and started walking toward the Habitat. The hamster crawled over to the dress, sniffed it, turned up its nose, and ran off to join the other hamsters.

"Well!" said Rarity, disappointed. It wasn't often that someone, even a hamster, turned down one of her stylish creations.

Meanwhile, Fluttershy had carefully created a trail of food pellets across the room. But the hamsters weren't even eating them. They were picking them up and pelting one another with them. It was nuts. They were out of their minds!

Fluttershy went and grabbed her

* * 73 * *

backpack and began searching through it for something that might help her lure the hamsters back to their Habitat. She found a can of cat food and set it aside. She pulled out some dog treats that were bigger than the hamsters themselves. She found an old tambourine from when she was little and turned it over in her hands. Maybe she could use it as a scoop and catch the hamsters one by one with it!

Rarity had taken out a bolt of cloth from her backpack and was trying to use it as a net. She threw it over a large group of hamsters, but they just scurried out from beneath it. Rarity was waving her giant piece of cloth, Fluttershy was trying to use her tambourine as a scoop, and the hamsters were evading both of them. Rarity and Fluttershy were running in circles, the hamsters were jumping over their feet, and the next thing the girls knew they had bumped into each other. *Bam!* Rarity threw the bolt of fabric over Fluttershy's head, blinding her, and completely surprised, Fluttershy began shaking the tambourine wildly.

All the hamsters stopped, mesmerised.

But the moment Fluttershy took the fabric off her head, she stopped jingling the tambourine. The hamsters began fighting again. Fluttershy experimented and shook the tambourine gently. At the first tinkling of the tambourine, the hamsters were rapt, gazing up at her, silent and obedient. She shook it a little more, and they began to walk toward her. As she slowly slapped it against her leg in a steady beat, they started marching. They were hypnotised by the sound. Amazed, Fluttershy looked up at Rarity.

"Don't stop now, dear," begged Rarity. "You've found your audience!"

Fluttershy began to really play the tambourine, shaking and slapping it in a slow, hypnotic rhythm. Delighted by her music's effect, Fluttershy began to spin and dance toward the Habitat as she played. The hamsters followed in a straight line behind her.

Her music became wilder as she danced. As if by magic, a tail and ears appeared on Fluttershy. She was ponying up! She was carried away by the enchantment of it all.

Rarity followed behind, gently humming to the music.

One by one, the hamsters weaved past Fluttershy and quietly crawled back into their Habitat. Finally, when the very last hamster was inside and the door to the cage was sealed, Fluttershy dropped her tambourine and collapsed. Her tail and ears disappeared.

She was in a state of shock. It wasn't just the effect the music had on the hamsters, but the effect it had on *her*. She'd actually played an instrument of her own. "But would anyone want a tambourine in a band?" She didn't mean to say it out loud, but she did.

"That would be wonderful!" exclaimed Rarity. "All the best bands have tambourine players."

"They do?" questioned Fluttershy.

"They do!" said Rarity.

"I've been worried that I didn't have an instrument to play..."

"But you do, darling," Rarity reassured her.

"But I'll still have to perform in front

of the whole school..." she said nervously.

"You think that's going to be harder than playing for this audience?" Rarity pointed at the Habitat.

"Maybe you're right!" Fluttershy laughed. "If I get stage fright, I'll just imagine everyone is a hamster!"

Rarity was looking through one of the transparent tubes at Carl, who had managed to remove his scarf at last. "I never would have guessed hamsters would be so touchy about fashion," she sighed. "I guess there is such a thing as *too* fabulous."

"Not for the Equestria Girls!" said Fluttershy. "I can't wait to see the outfits you are going to create for our band!" She was so excited now, excited and relieved. What a great day it had turned out to be despite Rarity's hamster catastrophe.

"You know I've actually had fashion

shows go worse than this," Rarity confided to Fluttershy as they headed out the door of the Animal Rescue Centre. "As models go, hamsters are pretty low maintenance."

CHAPTER 10

Pinkie on the One

Pinkie Pie was obsessed with the Spring Fling. It was all she could talk about. How should they decorate the gym? What kind of banners should they make for the teams? How much glitter did they need? Oh, there was never enough glitter!

But there was one thing Pinkie Pie wasn't focusing on – and that was the band.

"What instrument do you want to

play?" asked Rarity.

"I don't know!" she said. "I'll think of something. Do you think we should do a Hawaiian theme for the dance or something more unusual, like outer space? You know, The Spring Fling Is Out of This World?"

"We don't have much more time left," said Rainbow Dash. "For the band."

The girls had been practising all afternoon at Canterlot High. Rarity had written some great lyrics, and Rainbow Dash had created unforgettable melodies to go along with them. Applejack had put it all together, and even Fluttershy had been having fun, harmonising backup vocals and adding a dash of fun with her tambourine. But something was missing from their sound. What was it?

Finally, the girls took a break and

joined Granny Smith in the kitchen of the school, where she was mixing up batches of cookies as treats. The girls crowded around while she stirred the batter, hoping for a bite of cookie dough or a lick of the spoon. What they were getting, however, was a lesson in baking.

"Just remember," said Granny Smith. "The most important thing about Sugar Butter Cocoa Cookies is to fold the batter."

"Fold it?" giggled Pinkie Pie. "Like a shirt?"

All the girls laughed.

"No," said Granny Smith, using the same tone of voice Rainbow Dash had when she was trying to get Pinkie Pie to settle down. "Foldin's baker talk. It means gently stir it, slowly. Too much arm turning'll make your cookies tougher than a lump of coal."

Granny Smith handed Pinkie Pie the bowl of batter before she went into the pantry to get some vanilla. Slowly, rhythmically, Pinkie Pie concentrated on stirring the batter this way and that.

"C'mon, Pinkie," said Rainbow Dash, exasperated. "We don't have time to make cookies. We need to focus on the band. We need to figure out what's the matter with it."

"I guess I could fold a *little* faster," said Pinkie Pie. With that, she took another bowl and another whisk and simultaneously folded both sets of batter. She began slowly at first, but soon her hands were flying as the whisks flicked back and forth in her nimble fingers. She was a whir of motion, flicking the whisks, tapping spoons on the counter, and sending the bowls spinning round and round in circles.

"Whoa there!" said Granny Smith, coming back into the kitchen. "That's not folding. That's drumming!"

Rainbow Dash's eyes lit up. She took Rarity aside and whispered to her, "Most people don't know how hard it is to find someone who can use both hands the way a drummer does."

"Do you think Pinkie Pie has the concentration to be a drummer?" Rarity wasn't so sure their flighty friend could focus on anything that didn't involve streamers and balloons.

Pinkie Pie had returned the batter bowls to Granny Smith but found some metal pans and spoons and begun clashing and banging and tapping them in a catchy array of snappy rhythms.

"She just might!" said Rainbow Dash.

"And that's what's missing from our band...a drummer!"

Later on, when Granny Smith took the cookies that Pinkie Pie had stirred out of the oven, the girls came back to the cafeteria, lured by their delicious smell.

"Well now," said Granny Smith. "These look near perfect!"

Pinkie Pie beamed with pride as Granny picked up a cookie and took a bite. Ouch! She nearly lost a tooth they were so hard.

"And I mixed them in half the time!" said Pinkie Pie proudly.

Granny Smith rubbed her jaw.

"Don't worry," said Applejack. "Pinkie Pie might not have what it takes to be a baker...but we've got some other plans for her particular skills!"

CHAPTER 11

Drumroll
Please

Pinkie Pie was in charge of the team decorations for the Spring Fling (of course!) and she'd organised all the girls in the locker room to decorate banners. She unfurled a huge roll of bulletin board paper and began painting the words *Go Team!* in huge, curly letters.

Rainbow Dash was sitting on one of the benches blowing up balloons, but what she was really doing was trying to convince

Pinkie Pie that she had what it took to be a drummer. "A drummer can't be just anybody," she explained to her.

That was why bands were always having trouble with their drummers. They often were people with too much energy – just like Pinkie Pie!

"Oh, of course not," responded Pinkie Pie, but she wasn't really listening. She had outlined the words on the banner in black paint and used all kinds of bright colours to fill them in, but they just weren't, well, *sparkly* enough.

"Now, it's important that our banner shine from the field," said Rarity, "all the way to the top of the stands."

"Yes!" agreed Pinkie Pie. "It's got to shine, shine, shine!"

"So feel free to use as much glitter as you want," suggested Rarity.

Pinkie Pie's eyes lit up! No words ever made her happier than those! You could never have enough glitter. She ran out of the locker room without saying another word.

"Do you think you can convince her to be our drummer?" asked Fluttershy. She had her tambourine with her and practised with it in every spare moment. Each time its disks jingled, some of her animal friends would poke their heads out of her backpack to enjoy the music.

"Rainbow Dash sure is tryin'!" said Applejack. "But Pinkie Pie don't seem to be gettin' the message."

Rarity leaned back against the lockers. "Don't worry about it too much. I think she will. She's a natural."

Pinkie Pie zipped back into the locker room with an absolutely giant jar of glitter in her hands. It was as big as a conga drum!

Pinkie twirled and whirled around the banner, beating the bottom of the jar to swirl the glitter across the banner. The other girls snapped their fingers and clapped their hands to the beat she was creating.

"A drummer has to have the right... instincts...you know," said Rainbow Dash with a wink to the other girls.

"Absolutely!" said Rarity.

"You betcha!" said Applejack.

"Of course," said Fluttershy.

"Totally!" agreed Pinkie. But she wasn't really listening. She was too busy applying more glue and more glitter to the banner until a sparkly cloud filled the whole locker room.

When it came time to bring the banner

out to the baseball field, it was so stiff they couldn't even roll it up. The girls had to carry it over their heads like a board to the tunnel where the players would emerge from their locker rooms, bursting through the banner as they did so.

Rarity was a little worried about that. She rapped her hand against the glitter-filled banner. "Pinkie, dear, exactly how much glitter did you use?"

"As much as I could!" exclaimed Pinkie happily.

Just at that moment, the baseball team charged out of the tunnel for the opening of the Spring Fling games. But instead of tearing through the banner, it stopped them like a brick wall, or rather, a wall made out of metal glitter. *Boom! Boom! Boom!* One after another, they hit it and bounced back into the tunnel.

"Oh well," shrugged Pinkie Pie. "Maybe I shouldn't have used quite so much glitter!"

CHAPTER 12

Snared!

All across the cafeteria, kids were talking about the Spring Fling. Word had got out that the Equestria Girls were going to perform.

"Rainbow Dash is an amazing guitarist. I heard her at the Music Centre," said one boy waiting in the lunch line.

"Applejack rocks the bass!" said his friend. "Even in a banana suit!"

"Wait until you hear Rarity on

keyboards. She's been playing for years," gossiped a group of girls at a table near the windows.

"And Fluttershy is their secret weapon," whispered one of her friends. "I've heard she can hypnotise people with her music."

"There's only one teensy-weensy problem." Trixie smirked, sitting down with them. "They don't have a drummer from what I hear. Every band needs a drummer. Whoever heard of a band without a drummer? Now, if you're a solo performer like the Great and Powerful Trixie, all you need is yourself…but having only part of a band? That's just no good, no good at all. It's too bad, really."

Across the cafeteria, Pinkie Pie was finished with her lunch and was excitedly tapping the table with her fork and spoon. *Tap tap tappa tap. Tappa tappa tap tap.*

Rainbow Dash opened up a bag of crisps and offered them to all the girls before taking one herself. "The thing about the drummer we get is that she's got to be someone with a lot of energy. A lot of energy. A whole lot."

"Absolutely!" agreed Pinkie Pie.

All the girls looked at her expectantly.

Pinkie Pie began clinking her fork against a glass. *Plink plink plink.* She tapped the table, *tap tap tappa tap,* plinked the glass, *plink plink plink, tappa tappa tap tap.* She wasn't paying any attention to the other girls at all. At all.

"I mean," continued Rainbow Dash more emphatically, "a LOT of energy. Enthusiasm. A drummer has to be able to carry the whole band on his, I mean her, shoulders."

The vibration from Pinkie's fidgeting

was shaking the entire table. Sandwiches were wiggling, water was splashing, and trays were sliding back and forth.

Tap tap tappa tap, plink plink plink went Pinkie's fork and spoon.

"Pinkie!" shouted Applejack, trying to get her to listen.

Pinkie Pie froze. "What?" she asked innocently.

Applejack just shook her head and laughed. Pinkie Pie went right back to her fork-and-spoon percussion session.

Rarity placed a calming hand on Pinkie Pie's arm. "We have got to find an outlet for all that energy, dear," she said sweetly.

All the girls nodded in agreement.

"Like what?" asked Pinkie.

"I think you need a drum set," suggested Rarity.

"But I don't know how to drum," said Pinkie Pie.

"Yes, you do!" said all the girls together. "You never stop!"

The girls put away their trays and threw away their rubbish and hurried out of the cafeteria to take Pinkie Pie to the music room.

"You're just going to try it," said Rainbow Dash.

"You'll see, darling. You'll be great at it," Rarity told her.

With a hyper mixture of excitement and nervousness, Pinkie Pie took a seat behind the drum set in the music room. She picked up the drumsticks and tapped the cymbals. They reverberated through the room, and she giggled.

"Do it just like in the cafeteria," encouraged Fluttershy.

Pinkie Pie started pumping the drum pedal, tickling the snare, and tapping out a tight rhythm on the bass drum. Quickly, she grooved into a tight trot, racing her sticks over the drums and creating ricocheting rhythms. Wow! She was wild! All she'd needed was the right instrument! *Clash!* went the cymbals. *Boom!* went the drum. The beat was galloping now, wilder and wilder. Pinkie Pie was a force of nature! Her hands were dancing, her feet were pumping, and her hair was flying. Her tail flipped as she swayed to the groove. Ears appeared. She was ponying up!

"This. Is. GREAT!" she shouted over the roar of her drum solo.

Rarity winked at Rainbow Dash. "Whatever made you think that Pinkie Pie would be good on the drums?"

Rainbow Dash giggled. "I don't know. Guess I just have a sense of these things!"

CHAPTER 13

Player Piano

The school bell rang at the end of the day, and the kids poured out of the building, headed to sports practice and band practice and to get their outfits ready for the Spring Fling. The Equestria Girls were having one last rehearsal before their debut. That is, if Rarity showed up. Where could she possibly be? Had she forgotten? Could she really think that working on her dress was more important than practising together?

Of course not.

Halfway across campus, Rarity was trying to get an enormous grand piano down the hall. She pushed. She shoved. She pulled. She groaned and moaned. But it just wouldn't move. Still, there was no way she was going to give up. No way!

"Rarity," she scolded herself. "Your friends are depending on you. You simply must get this piano to band practice. And that means making the impossible possible!"

She backed away from the piano and then charged at it at full speed, shoving it with all her might. It budged an inch. Maybe not even that much.

"Ugh!" moaned Rarity, collapsing on the floor. "I should have known Trixie was up to no good when she oh-so-generously offered to lend me her piano."

But Rarity hadn't been able to resist. Playing a grand piano with the band would look so magnificent. And it would sound so much better than that old upright in the music room she'd been using. But why was it so hard to move?

"What kind of person doesn't put a piano on wheels?" she asked herself. (But maybe she should have wondered what kind of person would take the wheels off a piano before suggesting one of the Equestria Girls use it.)

Rarity leaned her back against the piano, braced her legs, and pushed. Nothing. She got down on her hands and knees and grabbed hold of one of the piano's legs and pulled. Nothing. She sat on the floor and wrapped her arms around the pedals and tried to scoot it forward. It just wouldn't move.

Sweat was pouring down her face. Her skirt was ripped. Her hair was completely lank and flat. She stood up and, in a state of sheer frustration, banged her hand down on the keys. Her nail chipped.

Oh! That was the final straw. Not only couldn't she get the piano to practice, but she was going to have to play with ugly nails. She felt defeated. Tears welled up in her eyes and spilled down her cheeks.

"Just look at me!" she wailed. "I'm a... mess!"

What was she going to do? Her phone was dead, so she couldn't call her friends, everyone had already left the school, and she was just so flustered. "And worst of all, I'm not the kind of girl that thinks it's fashionable to be fashionably late!"

That's when the Diamond Dog boys

appeared. They certainly weren't on any teams or involved in any clubs. They usually spent the afternoons lurking around looking for trouble. *Well, today they can spend it moving a piano,* thought Rarity. *Because what Rarity needs is just a little more muscle.*

Her eyes sparkled as she straightened her clothes, wiped the sweat off her brow, and quickly ran a brush through her hair. She took a deep breath and exhaled, letting go of all her fury and frustration so that she would look as lovely as possible.

She leaned elegantly against the piano, posing. "Oh, boys!" she trilled. "Do you think you could lend me a hand?"

The boys looked around the empty hallway, and their eyes lit on Rarity. They grinned. It wasn't every day a girl as pretty as Rarity paid attention to them! They lumbered over to her, ready to help her with whatever she needed. But they didn't count on having to move a grand piano!

Rarity sent them off for rope and then arranged herself comfortably on the top of the piano. After all, it would be a lot easier to direct them from there, and she wouldn't get in their way.

Even three such strong boys with ropes had a hard time manoeuvring that enormous grand piano. But Rarity made sure to offer them lots of encouragement.

"I simply cannot thank you enough," she gushed as they grunted and groaned. "Do you boys work out?"

The boys blinked up at her and smiled. Rarity batted her long eyelashes at them, waving her hand down the hallway to make sure they kept on with their work. "I must say," she continued. "I'm terribly impressed! So manly! And while I am a bit repulsed by your musky smell," she held her nose daintily, "I can appreciate that you are diamonds in the rough."

They beamed at Rarity, full of pride and happy to be able to lend her a helping hand. *Diamonds in the rough*, that's exactly what they were. Rarity had said so!

The boys struggled to get the piano around the corner and came to the front entranceway of Canterlot High. Kids were milling around talking to one another, and the boys struggled to weave in and out of the crowd. Rarity stood up on the piano directing traffic.

"Excuse me! Pardon me!" she exclaimed as politely as she could. "Pardon me! Excuse me! Excuse us!"

But no one seemed to be listening. Ever resourceful, Rarity put her fingers in her mouth and whistled as loud as she could. And it was loud! Instantly the kids cleared in either direction.

"Thank you!" said Rarity.

The boys pulled the piano through the lobby and headed down the hallway that led to the music practice rooms. Rarity held her hand to her forehead like a sailor at sea looking for shore at last.

"Almost there, boys," she said encouragingly as they heaved and hoed.

Unfortunately, every door in the long hallway was shut, and Rarity couldn't remember exactly which practice room the girls were meeting in. She tried to listen, but she didn't hear a guitar or a drum or even a giggle.

"Now which classroom was it?" she wondered aloud. "I guess we'll just have to look in them all!"

The boys pulled Rarity and the piano in and out of one practice room after another, crisscrossing the hallway.

"Not that one," said Rarity, disappointed. "Nope. Sorry. So sorry. But we're getting closer. I'm sure of it!"

Meanwhile the Equestria Girls were getting worried. Pinkie Pie had set up her drum kit and couldn't stop fiddling with it. She'd bang the cymbals, startle Fluttershy, apologise, and then instantly bang them again. Rainbow Dash was pacing back and forth. Applejack kept tuning her bass. "Ugh! Where's Rarity?" said Rainbow Dash for the hundredth time.

"That gal prob'ly just wants to make some sorta grand entrance," said Applejack, shaking her head.

Just at that moment, the door burst open, and the exhausted, sweaty Diamond

Dog boys pulled the grand piano into the practice room. Rarity was draped across it, refreshed, relaxed, and ready to play music.

"Ta-da!" she announced.

"Told you." Applejack laughed.

CHAPTER 14

Keyboard Magic

Rarity's grand piano filled the entire music room. Pinkie Pie's drum kit was now pushed against the wall. Fluttershy was squished into the corner. Even worse, there was barely any room for the girls to stand, much less dance around while they sang.

Rainbow Dash squeezed around the piano. "Rarity, couldn't you have chosen a more . . . *portable* instrument?"

"Heavens no!" said Rarity, carefully

climbing off the top of the piano. She smoothed her skirt. "The grand piano is the most refined and elegant of instruments. With it, I will be able to express my full musicality."

The girls just looked at her, dumbfounded.

"Well, that's what Trixie said," explained Rarity.

"No wonder!" said Rainbow Dash.

"Now don't that beat all," agreed Applejack. "That gal only understands one thing and it's the—"

"Great and Powerful Trixie," said all the other girls together.

Rarity looked embarrassed, and she began running her hands over the piano keys, practising some scales. "It does make a lovely sound…"

Rainbow Dash glanced at her watch,

sighing. "Well, that's nice, but our time here is up. We have to move to our other rehearsal space." She picked up her guitar and her amp. She let out another big sigh as she looked again at the grand piano.

"Guess you're gonna express your full musicality across campus."

"What?" Rarity looked alarmed. All the frustration of the afternoon came back. She couldn't go through moving the piano one more time. It was just too much. "No!" she wailed.

Pinkie Pie's eyes had been darting around the room. All at once they sparkled! She began jumping up and down and clanging the cymbals. She waved her drumsticks in the air! She had a solution! Oh boy, did she ever!

"Or you could play this!" she announced, reaching for a strange-looking guitar that was sticking out of the music room cupboard. She held it over her head.

It had the white and black keys of a traditional keyboard, but a tuning arm and a strap just like a guitar. All the girls gazed at it, stunned, especially Rarity.

"It's part guitar and part keyboard. It's a…a…guitarkey!" announced Pinkie Pie, jumping up and down with excitement again.

"A keytar," corrected Rainbow Dash, who knew her musical instruments, even if she'd never actually seen one of them before.

Pinkie shrugged. "Potato, tomato." With a big, enthusiastic smile on her face, she handed the keytar to Rarity like it was a Christmas present. She squealed delightedly as Rarity slowly strapped the instrument around her neck.

The girls stepped back to give Rarity some room. She fumbled with the control panel for a moment until she found the ON switch. She touched one of the keys. It had a powerful and precise sound. A little surprised, she grinned as she began trying out a scale. She wasn't used to playing the keys from this position, but she was a talented player.

With one hand, she began finding the melody of a song while the other girls added the beat. The giant sound of the keytar filled the room. Rarity's fingers were dancing across the keyboard, her whole body swaying to the music. What was great about the keytar was that she could dance while she played, just like Rainbow Dash and Applejack. She swirled, she turned, she grooved, she rocked! She ponied up!

First her ears appeared and then her tail. The keytar helped her make music magic.

"Oh my!" she sang as she danced.

"Cool!" shouted Rainbow Dash.

"Will ya look at that!" exclaimed Applejack.

"Oh my goodness!" said Fluttershy.

But most amazed of all were the Diamond Dogs. They'd never seen or heard anything like it before. Their mouths were wide open. They were on the floor! If they'd been hypnotised by Rarity before, now they were absolutely mesmerised.

"What do you think, fellas?" Rarity winked as she finished off her solo with a final flourish and returned to normal. "Did I make those ears and tail work for you or what?"

Still unable to talk, the boys nodded their heads.

Applejack put an arm around Rarity. "Looks like your *full musicality* does just fine with a keytar. What do you say to keepin' it on and movin' your tail to our next rehearsal space?"

"Fine, fine," said Rarity, running a hand over her keytar. She loved it. It was so much more fun to play than a piano, especially in a band. But what was she going to do with the piano now? She had to return it to the room she'd borrowed it from, didn't she?

She sashayed over to the Diamond Dogs and put an arm around them. She batted her eyes and smiled at them. "I probably should return that piano to Trixie..." she said.

The boys just stared at her, waiting.

"I don't suppose…" Rarity said in her sweetest voice.

The boys fell over one another to do one more thing for Rarity, and together they pushed and pulled and tugged the piano out of the room.

Rarity grinned. "I thought they might."

The afternoon had worked out so much better than she thought! And now she had her beloved keytar to play!

CHAPTER 15

School of Rock

DJ Pon-3 arrived early to school the next day. There were so many things to do before the Spring Fling that night. But the moment she opened the front door of Canterlot High, she heard music, incredible music, music that made her want to dance. Someone had gotten to school even earlier than she had.

The Equestria Girls! They were practising their instruments and filling the school with their rockin' tunes!

All the kids who were usually gossiping and doing homework in the main lobby were tapping their feet and swaying to the music. DJ Pon-3 noticed that everyone seemed happy, like they were about to start dancing. A girl bounced by with her books in her arms, and she was doing the Pony Stomp without even realising it. Some boys rushed past on their way to their lockers, and they were strutting their stuff and snapping their fingers.

DJ Pon-3 felt like she'd walked onto the set of a music video!

"Hey, hey, everybody,
We're here to shout,
That the Magic of Friendship
Is what it's all about!"

The music followed her down the hallway to her first class. Students were opening and closing their lockers to the beat. They shuffled their books from hand to hand like it was a dance move. Girls put on lipstick at their lockers and brushed their hair, all in time to the singing of the Equestria Girls. Even the teachers were getting into it!

Cranky Doodle was storming down the hallway in his usual grumpy mood when, all of a sudden, he jumped up in the air, did a split, landed, twirled, and opened the door to his classroom, singing and smiling.

DJ Pon-3 danced into class behind him and put her books down on her desk. Behind her she heard a whirring noise in time to the music. It was the classroom hamster, and even he was dancing on his running wheel. The bells of Fluttershy's tambourine were working their magic!

Up at the front of the class, her teacher had set up a science experiment, and each bubble that burst out of the test tube seemed to be part of the whole musical experience.

DJ Pon-3 sat down at her desk and happily watched the rest of the kids pour into the classroom, bopping and singing.

But then the bell rang, and the music suddenly stopped.

Now the kids in class just seemed noisy. Someone threw a paper airplane across the room. Another kid flung a spitball. Cranky Doodle yelled at them. Some gossiping girls laughed obnoxiously. A kid leaned back in his chair and it scraped against the linoleum, making a squeaking noise. Every little sound was noticeable to DJ Pon-3, and none of the sounds seemed happy.

A boy blew his nose. A girl unzipped her backpack. Someone crumpled up a piece of paper.

The teacher was just scraping a piece of chalk across the board when the fire alarm blared. *Whan! Whan! Whan!*

Vice Principal Luna appeared in the doorway. "Everyone get in line. Class is delayed. We're having a practice fire drill."

Quietly, the kids got into a line and marched out of the classroom, down the hallway, and through the back door. The only sounds were footsteps. Class after class filed outside. Teachers were taking the register.

But outside on the grass in the sunshine, someone began humming the tune from that morning. Another student joined in. Soon everyone was singing along and dancing in place. It was an unforgettable song!

"When everyone hears *my* music, they are going to love it even more," said Trixie. "I'm going to be the star of the Spring Fling. Just you wait and see."

DJ Pon-3 pulled down her shades, typed out a text, and looked at Trixie. "The difference between you and the Equestria Girls, Trixie," it said, "is that *you* want to be the star, but the Equestria Girls know how to put their music in the spotlight. They let the music be the star. And that's why everyone loves it."

Just at that moment, all of Canterlot High erupted into song.

"Hey, hey, everybody,
We're here to shout,

That the Magic of Friendship,
Is what it's all about!"

CHAPTER 16

Music to our Ears!

The Equestria Girls had each found an instrument to play. They had written songs. They had practised. Rarity had sewn them all fantabulously stylish pony ears and tails for the big night. There was only one problem. They were ready for the Spring Fling – but the Spring Fling was *not* ready for them!

When they arrived with their gear to set up at the gym, they opened the doors to discover a pastel pink paradise. There were pink balloons and pink streamers. There was a big bowl of pink lemonade sitting on a pink tablecloth. It would have been perfect for a sleepover, Pinkie Pie's sleepover that is, but it did not set the mood for a high school dance party. Not at all!

"Isn't it fun and silly?" Pinkie Pie giggled. "I decorated it this afternoon!"

None of the girls knew what to say. They didn't want to disappoint Pinkie Pie after all of her hard work, but...

Rainbow Dash sighed.

Fluttershy looked down at the floor, tears welling up in her eyes.

Applejack coughed.

Rarity spoke up at last. "It's so pretty, Pinkie Pie," she said. "Just like you. But we want something a little more—"

"Hawaiian?" interrupted Pinkie Pie. "I thought about doing a Hawaiian theme. I've even got tiki lamps and tropical flowers and leis to give out to the kids as they arrive. I could play the ukulele…"

"You've got to play drums," Rainbow Dash reminded her.

"Our sound just isn't Hawaiian exactly," said Rarity. "We need a more stylish flair. What if we turned the stage into a runway? We could add hats and boas to our costumes. I've got one right here." She pulled a long purple boa out of her backpack and swirled it around her neck. "We could do a fashion show while we're being a band!"

One of the feathers from the boa tickled Pinkie's nose and she let out an enormous sneeze. *Kerchoo!* Feathers flew everywhere!

Applejack spoke up now, suggesting a country theme. "And I'll make sure to have some of my apple juice delivered!" she said. "We'll deck the place out with hay bales and wagon wheels. We can even get a mechanical bull for the kids to ride. It'll be the best hoedown in town."

"Cool your spurs, Applejack," said Rainbow Dash. "We're a pop group, not country. I'd like to see us playing an arena at halftime one day. Look, we're already in a gym. Why not use the equipment we've already got? We can add an archery range, bring in some basketballs. It'll be awesome."

"It'll be gym class, not a dance," said Rarity.

Even Fluttershy had opinions about how to decorate the gym. "I've always wanted to set up a petting zoo here. We can decorate with pictures of all kinds of animals. We can even bring in pigs and sheep and goats for everyone to cuddle!" She clapped her hands. "And we can have a pet adoption centre…"

"I have a bunch of ideas I didn't use," said Pinkie Pie, jumping up and down. "And I've got all the decorations. We could do a pirate theme with treasure chests and sword fights! We could all wear eye patches and pirate hats. Yo ho ho!"

Pinkie Pie dashed over to the supply cupboard and started pulling out all kinds of enormous boxes. One of them was labelled PIRATE STUFF and draped with a skull-and-crossbones flag. Rarity picked it up and just shook her head.

But Pinkie Pie was on a roll. "Okay, so no pirates," she said without even catching her breath. "How about magicians?" She pulled open the top of another box and found a magic wand. "We could make it a tribute to Twilight Sparkle!"

"But she didn't do that kind of magic," said Rainbow Dash. "Twilight Sparkle is from beyond the stars. We need telescopes and astronaut costumes!"

"Absolutely not!" Rarity stomped her foot. "The stars are fine but no astronauts. I do think we need more glitter, though. Let's bedazzle the room with diamonds and a reflecting ball. Let's make it shimmer and shine."

Fluttershy blinked. "But no one likes it when it's too bright."

Tempers were beginning to flare. Rarity's face was turning unfashionably red. Fluttershy was blinking back tears. Rainbow Dash was tapping her foot. Applejack was shaking her head. And

Pinkie Pie was running around the gym pulling out more and more boxes.

"We could do a dentist's office...no? Okay then, how about an undersea theme? No? What about butterflies? You like butterflies, right, Fluttershy?"

"I do," she said tentatively. "But not for decorations."

"Worst. Party. Theme. Ever!" said Rainbow Dash.

"You girls having some trouble?" said Trixie, poking her head through the door. "I'd be happy to do your decorating for you. I have a ton of posters of the Great and Powerful Trixie we can put all over the walls..."

"No!" shouted all the Equestria Girls together.

"We're fine," said Rainbow Dash. "We know exactly what we are doing.

Goodbye, Trixie! See you tonight."
Rainbow Dash waited until Trixie had
disappeared before suggesting a new idea.
She looked at her friends and began
singing the tune they had all written
together.

"We've just got the day,
To get ready,
And there's only so much time to lose,
Because tonight,
Yeah, we're gonna party.
Now we'd better hurry up and choose!"

"What would Twilight Sparkle tell us if
she was here?" said Fluttershy.

"She'd say it was time for some
teamwork," said Applejack.

Trixie could be so irritating sometimes.
Still, her self-centredness had pointed out

something important to the girls about how they had all been behaving.

"How about we keep Pinkie Pie's balloons?" said Rainbow Dash.

Pinkie Pie clapped her hands with excitement.

"Serve up some of Applejack's special apple juice?"

Applejack slapped her leg, pleased as punch.

"Decorate the walls with pictures of Fluttershy's adorable animal friends?"

Fluttershy squealed with excitement.

"Add Rarity's diamond disco ball!"

"Yes!" exclaimed Rarity.

"And how about we include a little starlight magic as a tribute to Twilight Sparkle?"

"But there's nothing of yours in the decorations," said Fluttershy, concerned.

"Oh, but there is!" announced Rainbow Dash. "Look around! It's a rainbow of colours, just like me! So I win!" She laughed.

But all the other girls helped string together streamers in a rainbow pattern. It was always better when you worked together!

"Now, girls," said Rainbow Dash when they were done. "It's time to set up our instruments and play some music!"

CHAPTER 17

Dancing Room Only

The gym was packed! The lights of the disco ball twinkled and glittered. The boys had put on their best clothes, and the girls were all dressed up. Everyone was wearing pony ears and tails. They were the Canterlot Wondercolts, and this was their Spring Fling!

Up onstage, the Equestria Girls took their places. Rainbow Dash tuned her guitar one last time and checked her amp. Rarity limbered up her fingers. Fluttershy tried to remember that everyone on the gym floor was no more scary than her hamsters. Applejack gave a triumphant strum to her bass. It had never sounded so good!

Rainbow Dash grabbed a microphone. "Hey, Canterlot Wondercolts! How's everybody doing tonight?"

"What's up, Canterlot High?" sang out Pinkie Pie.

The crowd erupted into cheers. "Go, Equestria Girls!!!!"

"Hey, what about me?" piped up a voice from the back of the room. "The Great and Powerful Trixie is also performing. The Equestria Girls are just the warm-up band. I'm the STAR!"

"Who's in your band?" shouted someone.

"Yeah, where's your band?"

"Who's playing with you?"

"Who's your drummer?"

Trixie looked dumbfounded. She'd been so focused on herself that she'd forgotten that she needed a backup band!

"Don't worry, Trixie," said Fluttershy. "When the Equestria Girls have done with our set, we can play for you, too!"

Trixie stomped her foot. "Never! I'm the star! I'm going to be the only one onstage!"

Just then, she got another text from DJ Pon-3. "Tell you what, Trixie. First we'll hear from the Equestria Girls, and then you can play a song, and then the crowd can decide who they want to hear for the rest of the night!" it said. Trixie read the text aloud reluctantly.

The crowd roared its approval.

"C'mon, Equestria Girls! It's time to rock!" said Rainbow Dash.

Rarity introduced the melody with her keytar. Applejack started building in some rhythm with her bass. Rainbow Dash strummed her guitar, Fluttershy began to sway with her tambourine, and Pinkie Pie went wild on the drums.

"We don't know what's gonna happen!" sang Pinkie Pie.

"We just know it's gonna feel right!" crooned Rarity.

"All our friends are here, and it's time to ignite the lights!" answered Pinkie Pie.

Then all together the girls blasted out the chorus of their song.

"Shake your tail 'cause we're here
To have a party tonight!
Shake your tail! Shake your tail!"

The kids went wild! They were dancing and shaking and clapping and grooving. Everyone was doing the Pony Stomp. They crossed their arms at the elbows and bent from side to side. They lifted their knees and pranced. They jumped and clapped. They sang along with the Equestria Girls. Who could resist them? No one. Not even Trixie!

At first, she was leaning against the wall, her arms folded angrily, a sour expression on her face. But then her foot began tapping, and then her knees began lifting, and then she was swaying from side to side, and then she was dancing and prancing with everyone from Canterlot High. Even Trixie wanted to do the Pony Stomp!

Rainbow Dash burst out in a solo! *"So what if you didn't get it right the first time!"*

"Laugh it off!" sang Pinkie Pie, dazzling with her drums. *"No one said it's a crime!"*

"Do your thing!" sang Rarity, hitting the high notes. *"Yeah, you know you're an original!"*

"Your ideas are so funny that they're criminal!" harmonized Rainbow Dash.

"Oh YEAH!" sang the girls.

"Oh YEAH!" answered the crowd.

*"Shake your tail 'cause we're here
To have a party tonight!
Shake your tail! Shake your tail!"*

Everyone that night experienced the magic of the Equestria Girls' music, and no one wanted them to stop playing, not even Trixie. Especially not Trixie! At the very end of the night, she hummed to herself all the way home.

Far away in Equestria, Twilight Sparkle
was getting ready for a dance at the palace.
She was wearing her tiara and lots of
pretty jewels. Flash Sentry would be there,
and maybe she would dance with him. She
could hear guests arriving downstairs,
and a band starting to tune up. But
Twilight Sparkle could hear different
music, upbeat and friendly. It seemed to
be coming from the stars.

For a moment, Twilight Sparkle had a
vision of herself onstage in the gym at
Canterlot High. All the kids were there
wearing their pony ears and tails. Pinkie
Pie was going crazy on the drums.
Fluttershy was waving a tambourine.
Rarity's fingers were racing across a keytar,

and Rainbow Dash and Applejack were rocking their guitars. Twilight Sparkle wanted to be there, singing with her friends. She really did. Maybe one day. Maybe the magic would happen again.

As she pranced downstairs to her own party, she began singing the song she'd heard.

> *"Shake your tail 'cause we're here*
> *To have a party tonight!*
> *Shake your tail! Shake your tail!"*

Read on for a sneak peek
of the next exciting
Equestria Girs adventure,

The Mane Event

Teenagers streamed in and out of the fast-food restaurant next to Canterlot High School, happily chatting with their friends. They were talking about football practice and dance committees and gossiping about the newest couples. They were also buzzing about the Sonic Rainbooms' new song.

"A friend for life is what we want to be!" sang a cheerful group of girls strolling out of the restaurant. With chips and drinks in hand, the kids hurried off to do homework, waving goodbyes and texting last-minute messages. No one noticed the three bickering new girls who left the restaurant without buying a single thing to eat.

Adagio Dazzle, looking irritated, tossed her lush mane of pastel-colored hair. Aria Blaze let out a dissatisfied sigh that sounded just like a whinny, and Sonata Dusk stomped her foot, discovering that human shoes did not make the same satisfying clomp as pony hooves.

A wisp of fluorescent green light wove in between the girls as they slumped against one another. As it wound around their heads, each girl slightly opened her mouth and seemed to drink in a tiny sip of the strange light. For a moment, the scarlet pendant hanging around each girl's neck seemed to glow.

"That was barely worth the effort," complained Aria. "I'm tired of fast food.

I need a real meal."

"What did you expect?" said Adagio. "The energy in this world isn't the same as in Equestria. We can only gain so much power here."

Aria pouted and sighed again. "I wish we'd never been banished to this awful place!"

"Really?" said Adagio, her voice dripping with sarcasm. "I love it here."

"For realsies?" snipped Sonata. "Because I think this place is the worst."

"I think you're the worst, Sonata," Aria shot back at her.

Sonata's face turned red with fury. "Oh yeah? Well, I think you're worser than the worst, Aria."

"Yeah?" Aria turned her back on the other girls and stared out at the street. "I'm kinda busy right now. Can I totally ignore you some other time?"

Adagio practically snorted with rage. "I'll tell you one thing: Being stuck here with you two isn't making this world any more bearable."

Suddenly, underneath the normal evening noises of teenagers, cars, and music, each girl began to hear a strangely familiar hum. It was pleasingly pitched and just barely audible, so faint that no one else even realized it was there. But the girls heard it, and all three of them instantly turned toward the horizon.

That's when they saw it. In the distance, just beyond the fields of Canterlot High, was the faintest ripple of magical, rainbow light.

Adagio's eyes widened greedily. Beside her, Aria and Sonata were so thrilled they could barely breathe. The three girls were transfixed by the beautiful colours illuminating the sky.

Adagio was the first to speak. "Did you feel that?" she asked the other girls in a hushed voice. "Do you know what that is?"

The other girls couldn't bring themselves to admit it. How could it be? It wasn't possible.

But Adagio couldn't contain her excitement."It's . . . it's . . . Equestrian magic!"

Read
The Mane Event
to find out what happens next!

The Equestria Girls started their own band
by working together and putting their
best hooves forward! Turn the page
and dream up your own band,
just like Twilight Sparkle!

In the Band

List the names of your best friends and
an instrument that each one would
rock. Don't forget to include
a vocalist and a keytar player!

Pinkie Pie – Drums

_____

_____

_____

_____

_____

_____

_____

_____

Elements of Harmony

Why do you think you and your friends
work so well together? Write about your
Elements of Harmony and how they will
help your band succeed.

_____

_____

_____

_____

_____

_____

_____

_____

_____

A Major Makeover

If you and your friends started a band
and performed at the Spring Fling, how
would you make yourselves 20% cooler?
Would you have a band style?
Design it here!

Mane Name

Now that you have your band's image, it is time
to think of a name that fits the group!
First, list the names of your favourite bands!
(Don't forget the Equestria Girls!)

_____

_____

_____

_____

_____

_____

_____

_____

Next, list some possible names for your
band! Make sure the name matches
your unique sound.

_____

_____

_____

_____

_____

_____

_____

_____

_____

Lyrical Laughter

Below is a set of lyrics sung by the Equestria Girls at the Spring Fling! Use your lyrical talents to write the next verse!

"So what if you didn't get it right the first time!

Laugh it off!

No one said it's a crime!

Do your thing!

Yeah, you know you're an original!

Your ideas are so funny that they're criminal!"

In Need of a Tune-Up

Do you know anyone like Trixie – someone
who is competitive for the wrong reasons?
Someone who gets upset when
everything does not go his or her way?
Write about that person here.

_____

_____

_____

_____

_____

_____

_____

Have you ever acted like Trixie?
List some ideas of how you can be
competitive in a positive way!

Be proud of others' accomplishments,

not threatened.

Incognito Instruments

Can you help the Equestria Girls
by finding their missing names and
instruments in this word search?

```
B  A  T  H  B  K  T  D  S  S  Z  K  D  U  V
C  X  K  W  H  C  W  V  H  K  E  K  F  O  M
Q  I  X  S  I  V  O  S  P  Y  L  Z  E  I  A
C  J  S  G  M  L  A  R  T  H  H  G  S  F  N
U  A  E  K  N  U  I  A  A  S  M  G  G  A  R
B  J  I  A  Z  J  R  G  A  R  L  U  T  S  O
Y  M  P  K  X  W  Y  D  H  E  I  A  R  P  Q
J  D  E  B  W  X  W  C  S  T  O  T  C  K  O
E  N  I  R  U  O  B  M  A  T  X  P  Y  O  S
J  J  K  V  B  J  R  R  X  U  X  C  R  H  V
T  C  N  N  P  G  Z  B  T  L  B  A  V  D  B
V  E  I  B  Q  M  T  D  D  F  P  I  N  R  I
M  A  P  P  L  E  J  A  C  K  G  I  H  D  Z
R  H  Y  R  C  Z  E  I  Q  K  C  K  A  R  F
I  T  R  I  X  I  E  S  W  F  S  X  T  R  L
```

APPLEJACK

DRUMS

FLUTTERSHY

GUITAR

KEYTAR

PINKIE PIE

RAINBOW DASH

RARITY

TAMBOURINE

TRIXIE

TWILIGHT

VOCALS

Presto Poster

Create a couple of dazzling posters to get
Canterlot High excited about your band's
performance at the Spring Fling!